6.8.2022

Brightest burning flame. You provide warmth where ever you go. Keep providing warmth in times of cold. Keep loving! We need you.

Trace

Quick the Brown Fox

Copyright © 2011 by Prince G. Tebbs

All rights reserved. No part of this book may be reproduced or transmitted in any form or by any means without the written permission of the author/illustrator.

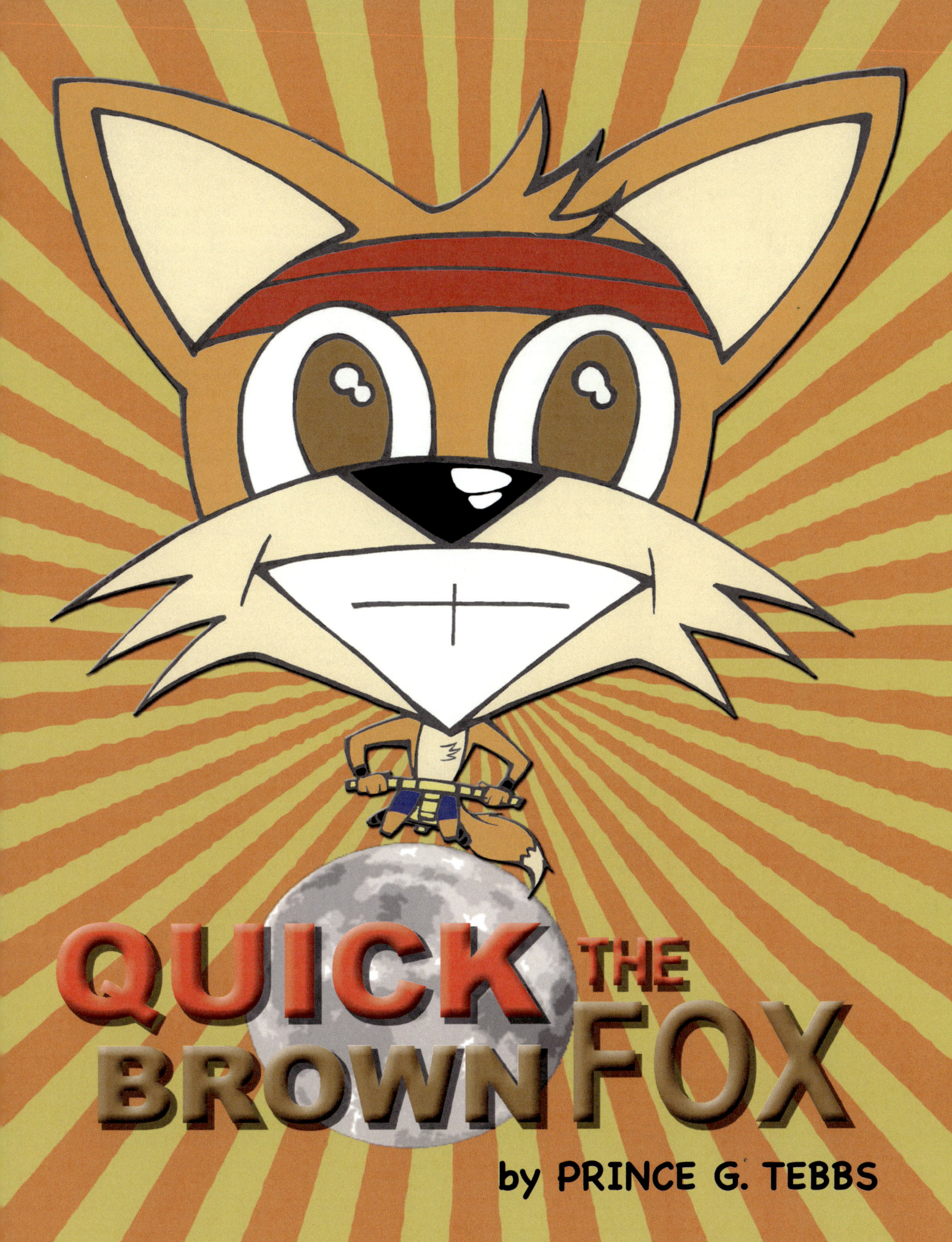

Special thanks and dedication to the late Amy Dunbar Tebbs. You always believed in me and encouraged me with teachable moments. I love you mommy.

BEFORE YOU BEGIN YOUR ADVENTURE WITH QUICK...

Congratulations on purchasing this book! We share the desire to start the learning process at an early age. Children are the future, our "good fruits" to make this world a better, brighter, and smarter place.

I would like to take a moment to welcome you to this wonderful book that is very dear to my family and I. My vision was to create a story that made learning to read fun. All fun aside, this book is about setting goals, being fearless and believing you can achieve what you set out to accomplish.

Nearly every page in this book contains activities and games to help your children become better readers. The story contains color-coordinated letters; the idea is to encourage your child to find all the letters, from A-Z, that are included on every page. Encourage your child to say the word they find the letter in. Play along! See who can find all the letters the fastest. Work along side them, teaching them the words the letters form and other words that start with the same letters. Maximize the learning experience with the additional activities like color recognition, rhyming, hidden words and more!

Have fun with this!

THIS IS QUICK. HE IS ONE ACTIVE BROWN FOX WHO LOVES TO JUMP OVER LAZY DOGS.

THIS IS WOOZY, A VERY LAZY DOG. HE DOES NOT CARE MUCH FOR QUICK BROWN JUMPING FOXES, BUT ONLY ABOUT SLEEPING.

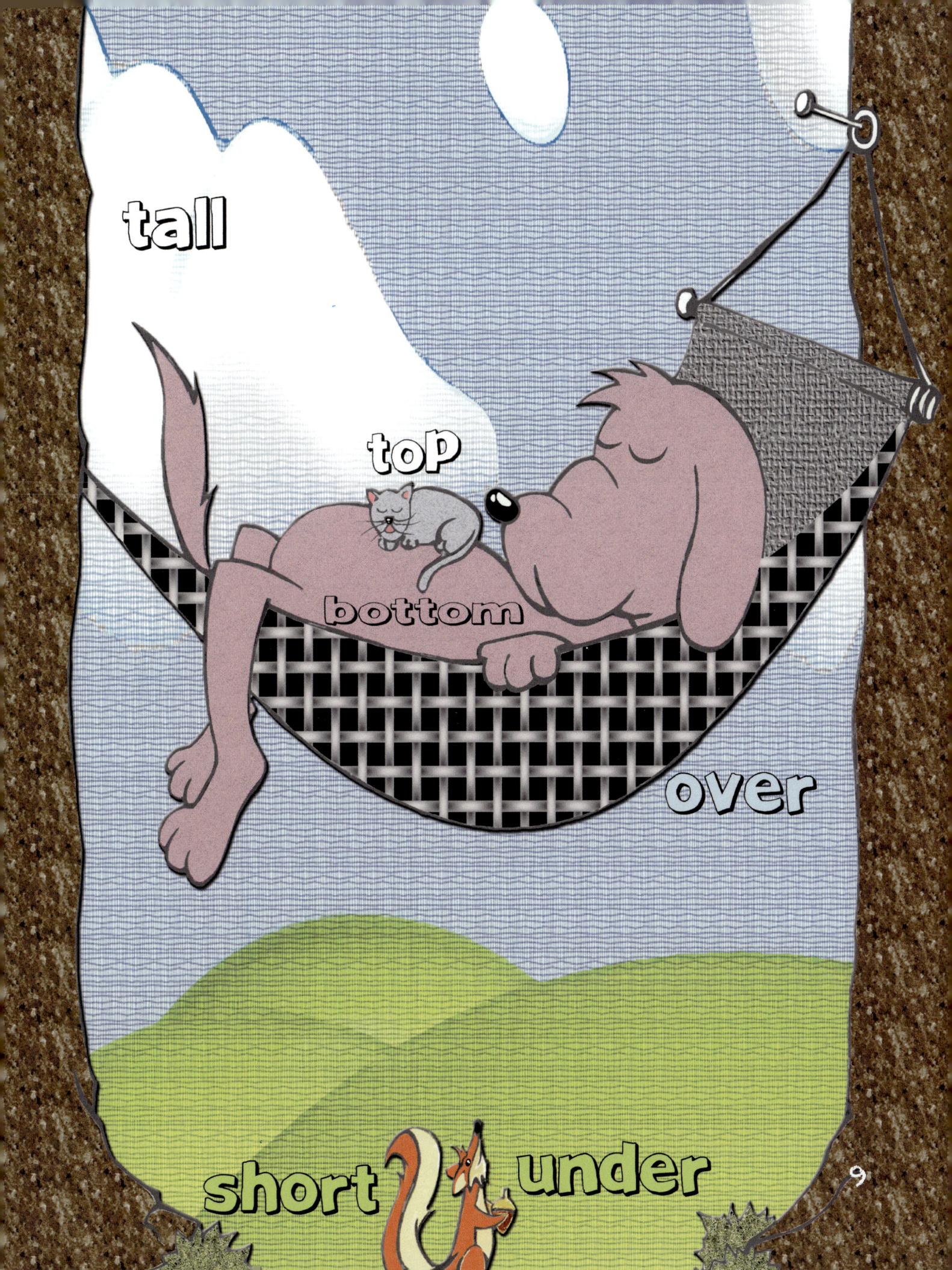

"WOOZY WOOZY," says Quick the Brown Fox.

"Stop being so lazy! All you ever do is sleep! Have an adventure with me just this once. I finally got that package I have been waiting for. Come and see what's in it."

"It's AWESOME!"

red

orange

brown

"NO THANKS"

"WOOZY LOOK!" says Quick the Brown Fox. "It's my new pogostick. With this I bet I can jump over ten lazy dogs."

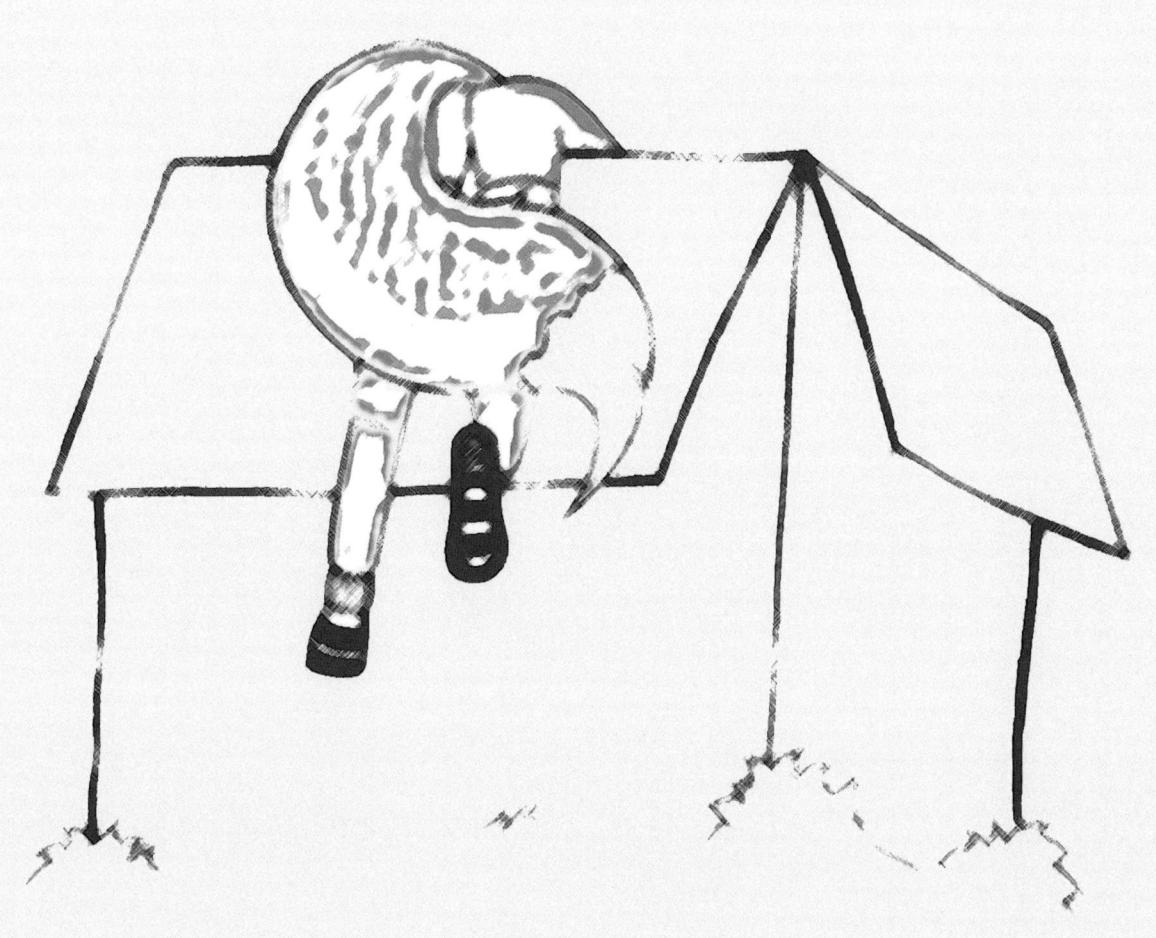

Which word rhymes with FOX?

POGOSTICK? JUMP? BOX?
TAIL? ROCKS? LAZY? SOCKS?

But that lazy dog
Woozy just snores and
dreams of lazier days.

"HERE I GO YOU LAZY DOG,"

"WITH A COUPLE QUICK HOPS I WILL JUMP RIGHT OVER YOU."

"MY NAME IS QUICK AND I HAVE PLANS TO BE THE HIGHEST JUMPING BROWN FOX IN ALL THE LAND."

What letters can you find? What words can you make?

SO QUICK THE BROWN FOX
JUMPED OVER THE LAZY DOG.

THEN QUICK THE BROWN FOX JUMPED SKY HIGH OVER THE TALL LAMP WITH A ZIG-ZAG POLE.

THEN QUICK THE BROWN FOX JUMPS OVER A GIANT LUNARMOTH LAZILY ZIPPING AND DIPPING THROUGH THE AIR.

QUICK THE BROWN FOX
WANTS TO JUMP EVEN HIGHER.

TO BE THE WIZ OF LEAP.
TO JUMP WITH EASE
PLEASANTLY AND DYNAMICALLY
OVER HEIGHTS.

WHEW! THAT WAS ALOT TO SAY.

N O P Q R S T U V W X Y Z

QUICK THE BROWN FOX BOUNCE

QUICK THE BROWN FOX POUNCE

QUICK THE BROWN FOX LUNGE

QUICK THE BROWN FOX SLUMPS

THEN QUICK THE BROWN FOX JUMPS

OVER THE LAZY MOON.

OVER THE GIANT LUNARMOTH.

OVER THE LAMP WITH A

ZIG-ZAG POLE.

AND OVER THE LAZY DOG.

WOW! QUICK THE BROWN FOX CAN SURE JUMP. HE DID IT. HE PUT HIS MIND TO IT HE DID IT. HE LET NOTHING STOP HIM!

BUT THAT LAZY DOG JUST ROLLED OVER AND CONTINUED TO SNORE BIG ZZZZZZS.

Don't be the lazy dog!
Be Quick the Brown fox.

Reach for the stars and grab as many as you can!

Your dreams are possible too.

Made in the USA
Middletown, DE
24 May 2022